THE CRUNCHBONE CASTLE CHRONICLES

KING CUDGEL'S CHALLENGE

by Karen Wallace
illustrated by Helen Flook

PICTURE WINDOW BOOKS
Minneapolis, Minnesota

J
WAL

Editor: Shelly Lyons
Interior Colorist: James Mackey
Page Production: Michelle Biedscheid
Art Director: Nathan Gassman
Associate Managing Editor: Christianne Jones

First American edition published in 2008 by
Picture Window Books
5115 Excelsior Boulevard
Suite 232
Minneapolis, MN 55416
877-845-8392
www.picturewindowbooks.com

First published in 2006 by A&C Black Publishers Limited, 38 Soho Square,
London W1D 3HB, with the title KING CUDGEL'S CHALLENGE.

Printed in the United States of America.

All books published by Picture Window Books
are manufactured with paper containing at least
10 percent post-consumer waste.

Library of Congress Cataloging-in-Publication Data
Wallace, Karen.
King Cudgel's challenge / by Karen Wallace ; illustrated by Helen Flook.
p. cm. — (Read-it! chapter books)
Summary: Twin siblings Princess Gusty Ox and Prince Marvin fight
constantly until the court wizard sends them on a challenge that requires
the royal pair to cooperate.
ISBN-13: 978-1-4048-3706-5 (library binding)
ISBN-10: 1-4048-3706-X (library binding)
[1. Fighting (Psychology)—Fiction. 2. Brothers and sisters—Fiction.
3. Twins—Fiction. 4. Princes—Fiction. 5. Princesses—Fiction.
6. Humorous stories.] I. Flook, Helen, ill. II. Title.
PZ7.W1568Ki 2007
[Fic]—dc22   2007004283

Table of Contents

Chapter One

In his dream, King Cudgel screamed and screamed. The sound that came out was something between a squeak and a whimper.

A mouse was nearby and pushed its furry face through the grass. "What's your problem?" it demanded angrily.

King Cudgel stared into a pair of hard beady eyes and realized, to his horror, that he was the same size as the mouse! No wonder he sounded so squeaky! No wonder no one had heard him calling!

He climbed onto a stone and shouted, "I am King Cudgel of Crunchbone Castle! I am ruler of this kingdom! Help!"

Suddenly, the ground shook, and two familiar voices filled the air. They sounded like fingernails scraping across a blackboard.

"It's my kingdom!" yelled Prince Marvin.

"No, it's not! It's my kingdom!" screamed Princess Gusty Ox.

King Cudgel froze with horror. Any minute now, his children would crush him underfoot. And they probably wouldn't even notice! Worst of all, he knew they wouldn't even care.

King Cudgel jumped down from his stone, looked at the mouse, and begged, "Can I hide in your nest? My children will—"

"Will you promise to stop squeaking?" interrupted the mouse.

"I promise," whimpered King Cudgel.

The ground shook with each step the children took. The terrible shouting grew louder and louder.

The mouse pointed up to a ball of woven straw attached to the long, stiff grass. "Help yourself!" the mouse said.

King Cudgel ran as fast as his tiny legs would carry him. He climbed the grass and curled up in the mouse's nest. A second later, the prince and princess thundered past, hitting each other with sticks and roaring like tigers.

Just then, the king's trusty servant looked at the ball of sheets that quivered on the royal four-poster bed. "Your Majesty," said Quail, in his calmest voice. "Wake up. You're just having a bad dream."

King Cudgel's spaniel, Fluffy, whined and pawed at the twisted pillowcases. Quail gently pulled at a corner of the curtain.

"A dream?" cried King Cudgel. He poked his nose above the bedsheets. "It's a nightmare, Quail!" he said. "And I have it every night!"

The king fell back on the pillows and said, "If I didn't have Fluffy to comfort me ... ." He closed his eyes.

"Is your nightmare about Prince Marvin and Princess Gusty Ox?" asked Quail. He stirred 10 sugar cubes into the king's mug of tea and put it down beside the royal bed.

King Cudgel opened his eyes and sat up. He grasped the mug in both hands and began to slurp.

"What am I going to do, Quail?" he asked. "Prince Marvin has never shared anything in his life, and Princess Gusty Ox wants everything for herself."

The king fished out the sugar cubes and stuck them in his mouth. He muttered, "I thought twins were supposed to get along. Why do mine fight all of the time?"

"You should never have told them you wanted to give up your kingdom and move to the seaside," replied Quail. He grabbed a damp cloth and wiped the king's fingers. Then he said, "It's only made things worse."

King Cudgel groaned. It was his dream to retire to a place of his own overlooking the sea. He had thought about it for a long time and had finally come up with the perfect name: *Sea View*.

His eyes traveled across the room to a portrait of his wife. She was an enormous woman with a face like a battle-ax and arms like huge sides of bacon. One day, she had picked up a walking stick instead of her sword and had gone out bear hunting. She had never returned.

"I wish Lady Carrion were here," the king sighed. "She's the only one who can stop the children from fighting, because she shouts louder than they do."

Quail looked at the portrait. His hands began to shake. Queen Carrion had been famous for her collection of bear skins. But she had been even more famous for her terrible temper. Crackle, the court wizard, once declared that he'd fainted as a result of her foul words.

King Cudgel grabbed a handful of sugar cubes from his emergency bedside chest and shoved them in his mouth.

"How can I retire when my children can't even share a bar of chocolate without tearing each other apart?" he wailed suddenly.

From the open window came a loud crack, as if someone had been hit over the head with a stick.

"The kingdom's mine," screamed the voice of Princess Gusty Ox.

"No, it's mine," snarled Prince Marvin.

"Stink Brain!" Gusty Ox replied.

"Elephant Feet!" yelled Marvin.

Then, there was a very loud splash, as if something, or someone, had been thrown into the moat. A second later, Prince Marvin squealed like a pig.

Quail shut the windows and drew the curtains again as the arguing continued.

It was the best he could do to block out the noise. If only some witch would come along and turn the children into stone, like they used to do in the old days. That would keep them from fighting!

Quail gasped. Why hadn't he thought of it before? King Cudgel didn't have a witch, but he did have a wizard!

"I've got it, sire!" Quail cried. "You should ask Crackle what to do."

King Cudgel leapt out of bed and shouted, "What a brilliant idea! Crackle will cast a spell to make my children stop fighting. Then they will share the kingdom, and I will retire to the seaside!"

Quail bowed and smiled proudly. "Shall I put out your favorite leopard-skin leggings and the jacket edged in purple feathers?" he asked. For despite the king's problems, he was always a flashy dresser.

16

"Yes indeed," cried King Cudgel. "Then summon Crackle. We'll settle this problem once and for all!"

Chapter Two

Princess Gusty Ox stomped around the forest, breaking tree trunks with both hands. It was something she did every morning to keep her arm muscles strong. She liked to keep fit. One day, she would be the queen of Crunchbone Castle, so she had to be strong enough to fight off intruders. And her brother, stink-brain Prince Marvin, was one of those intruders.

Suddenly, the ground gave away beneath her shoes, and she tumbled into a hole. The next minute, a nasty laugh floated above her, and the air was filled with something stinky.

"Got you!" cried Prince Marvin from the edge of the hole. "Now I'm going drop a snake on your head!" He grinned down at her and ran a skinny hand through his fine blonde hair. "Unless you promise to give me your share of the kingdom!" he said with an evil giggle.

"No way," muttered his sister. "You're nothing but a stink brain. You can't even lift an ax! You could never be king."

"At least I don't have elephant feet like you," snarled Prince Marvin. He dangled the snake in the air and asked, "Now, what's it going to be? Do I get the whole kingdom, or not?"

"You'd never have the guts to pick up a real snake," said Princess Gusty Ox, ignoring his question. "That's only a rubber one!"

"Wrong again, Elephant Feet!" cried Prince Marvin. He dropped the snake and ran away as fast as he could.

Princess Gusty Ox let out a howl of fury. She hated snakes! With one great heave, she was out of the hole and running after her brother, waving a big, fat stick.

As usual, Crackle, the court wizard, had turned himself into a frog. He was in the moat, sunning his belly on a lily pad, when Prince Marvin ran past.

Prince Marvin kicked a stone as he hurried past the moat. "Watch out, frog!" he yelled.

The stone hit Crackle on his froggy face. He hopped quickly out of the water.

A second later, Princess Gusty Ox appeared. She believed frogs were as bad as snakes. She tried to jump out of the frog's way, but her size-11 shoe headed straight for Crackle's leg.

Crackle moved quickly, but not quickly enough. The shoe caught his leg and knocked him back into the water.

At that moment, Quail appeared. Quick as a flash, Crackle turned himself back into a wizard and climbed out of the moat with as much pride as he could manage.

"There you are!" cried Quail. "I've been looking for you everywhere." He peered at the wizard's face and said, "That's a terrible black eye you've got."

"Just like the big bruise on my leg," muttered Crackle.

"Sunning yourself on a lily pad again?" replied Quail. "I warned you about that."

"Those children … ." Crackle said, rubbing his eye. "One day I'll straighten them out."

Quail took Crackle's arm. He helped the wizard hobble across the grass to the castle gates. "You might get the chance sooner than you think," he said. "The king has a job for you!"

Later, at the castle, King Cudgel looked at Crackle's rusty magic kettle. It didn't look magical to the king. "Are you sure this is going to work?" he asked.

"Of course it will, sire," replied Crackle. He filled the kettle with water and hung it over a small fire. "You'll see!" he said.

A few minutes later, steam poured out of the kettle's spout. The king watched as Crackle waved his magic wand and said something that sounded like *abracadabra!*

Suddenly, the steam formed a square. "Aha!" cried Crackle. "The magic window into the future." He peered into the square, and a great grin spread across his face.

King Cudgel looked over his shoulder. "What is it? I can't see anything," he said in a bad-tempered voice.

"Of course you can't, sire," replied Crackle. "You're not a wizard!"

"So, what is it?" asked Quail.

"The solution!" announced Crackle. "Sire, your nightmares are over!"

"Quail!" cried King Cudgel. "Summon Prince Marvin and Princess Gusty Ox! Tell them their kingdom is at stake!"

Princess Gusty Ox had Prince Marvin pinned to the ground. She was just about to jump on him when Quail showed up.

"Stop that immediately and come with me," he ordered. "Your kingdom is at stake!"

The princess turned and waved her fist in Quail's face. "Get lost," she snarled. "The only thing that matters is this fist, and it's about to hit my brother."

"Princess Gusty Ox," said Quail. "Your father commands your presence at once!

Unless you do as I say, you and your brother will lose your rights to the kingdom!"

The princess dropped her fist and climbed reluctantly off her brother. "If you're lying, Quail, I'll—"

"Oh, be quiet, Elephant Feet," muttered Prince Marvin. "It's my kingdom, anyway."

"No, it's not," replied Gusty Ox.

"Yes, it is," said Marvin.

"No," said Gusty Ox.

"Yes," replied Marvin.

"No," said Gusty Ox again.

It was unbearable. Quail put his fingers in his ears. "Follow me," he said. Then he walked quickly back to the castle door.

Chapter Three

"I'm not accepting a challenge!" snorted Princess Gusty Ox. She turned to Crackle. "I don't care what that wizard saw in his steam square."

"It's not fair," whined Prince Marvin. "Anyway, I don't like challenges."

Crackle had been expecting this to happen. He had advised the king to dress in his most important-looking clothes and wear

the biggest, spikiest crown he could find.

Now, King Cudgel stood up and held out his arms. "You will do as you're told!" he bellowed with as much power as he could muster from underneath his cloak.

The king looked into his children's faces and said, "If you don't accept my challenge, your cousin, Godric the Geek, will take over the kingdom when I retire."

Princess Gusty Ox and Prince Marvin stared at each other in horror. Godric the Geek was the most boring person in the entire kingdom. He knitted his own stockings. He liked arranging flowers. He even changed his clothes without being asked. The idea of Godric the Geek telling them what to do was absolutely awful. For a moment, the great chamber was completely silent. You could have heard a ghost whisper.

Princess Gusty Ox scuffed her shoe back and forth across the stone floor. Prince Marvin chewed a lock of his hair and pulled at a loose thread in his sleeve. Neither one of them wanted to budge, but they didn't have much choice.

"What do we have to do then?" asked Princess Gusty Ox at last.

It was Crackle's great moment. He leapt into the middle of the room and waved his wand in the air. Sparks flew out of his pointy hat, and a triumphant grin started to appear on his face.

"This is the challenge!" he cried. "First, you must find the golden pack of cards. Next, you must play the right game. Only then will you learn the secret that will give you the kingdom! You have three days to complete the task, and you must stay together all the time!"

Princess Gusty Ox and Prince Marvin looked at each other. Even though they disliked each other, they both agreed that anything was better than having Godric the Geek rule the kingdom.

The princess glared at Crackle. "OK, you frog-faced clown," she muttered. "When do we start?"

No one bothered saying goodbye to Princess Gusty Ox and Prince Marvin. Instead, they all began to celebrate. The idea that the castle would be peaceful for three whole days was too good to be true.

The royal children went down to the kitchen, where Quail had left them sandwiches for the first day. There was a note from Crackle that read, "After this, you're on your own."

Princess Gusty Ox trudged down a path in the forest, her big shoes sending shock waves through the ground.

At first, she decided to ignore Crackle's orders and stayed as far away from her brother as possible. Apart from everything else, she knew he had already eaten all of his sandwiches and would try to steal hers the moment she wasn't looking. Then she realized that if she lost him, they would lose the challenge, and Godric the Geek would get the kingdom.

Suddenly, Prince Marvin dropped from a tree branch and landed on Princess Gusty Ox's shoulders.

"This is all your fault!" he screamed.

"No, it's not!" yelled Princess Gusty Ox.

"Yes, it is!" cried Prince Marvin.

At once, the forest went dark, and a light appeared in the sky. Princess Gusty Ox and Prince Marvin looked up, and their hearts almost froze.

A picture of Godric the Geek hung above them, as if painted with stars. He was wearing the spiky Crunchbone crown, and there was a nasty smirk on his face.

Without a word, Prince Marvin slid off his sister's back, and they continued walking into the forest, side by side.

Soon, they came upon a river.

"It's too deep!" cried Prince Marvin, looking at the scummy river. "I can't swim!"

"Then how are you going to get across, Stink Brain?" asked Princess Gusty Ox.

"I'm not, Elephant Feet!" snarled Prince Marvin. "I'm going home!"

"You can't!" yelled Princess Gusty Ox. "You heard what Crackle said. We've got to do this together."

"Then you'll have to carry me!" the prince said as he glared at his sister.

"No way!" she replied.

In front of them, the water stirred. Something strange was happening in the scum. Bits of green weeds swirled into a picture. Godric the Geek appeared, and this time his smirk was even wider.

The princess bent down so her brother could climb onto her shoulders. "All right," she muttered. "But I still don't like you."

On the other side of the river, the ground was soft and swampy.

"There are no cards around here," whined Prince Marvin as he looked around.

"Maybe they're in a golden box that has sunk in the mud," said Princess Gusty Ox. She bent down on her hands and knees and started to feel around in the stinking slime.

Even though he felt sick, Prince Marvin

bent down and did the same. He couldn't
bear the idea that she might find the pack of
cards before he did.

All that day, the prince and princess
crawled through the smelly mud, feeling for
something hard and square. Mosquitoes
bit them. Flies tickled their noses. Beetles
crawled under their clothes and made them
itch all over.

At the end of the day, they pulled themselves out of the swamp and sat down against a wall. They were both too tired to wash the mud from their clothes, and they were too tired to fight over who smelled worse. They closed their eyes and quickly fell asleep.

The next day, they came to a field full of flat stones.

"Do you think the cards are under one of these stones?" asked Princess Gusty Ox.

"How should I know, Elephant Feet?" replied Prince Marvin. He picked up a stone and threw it at his sister's foot.

Princess Gusty Ox picked up a bigger stone and threw it at her brother. "Stink Brain!" she said as he yelped.

A huge swarm of wasps appeared in the sky like a black cloud. The prince and princess threw themselves on the ground and wrapped their arms around their heads. Then, peering through their fingers, they saw a truly terrible sight. The wasps had formed the shape of Godric the Geek, and the smirk on his face was wider than ever.

Prince Marvin got up and began to turn over stones as fast as possible. Instantly, Princess Gusty Ox was on her feet, too. But no matter how many stones they turned over, they found nothing.

At the end of the day, their fingers were cut and blistered, and their nails were torn. They slumped down by the trunk of a tall tree. They were too worn out and hungry to keep looking. They were even too tired to fight.

"We're going to lose the challenge," sighed Princess Gusty Ox.

"Maybe that's what Father planned," muttered Prince Marvin. "Maybe he really wants Godric the Geek to rule the kingdom."

"I think you're right," said the princess. "He hardly ever talks to us."

"He can't get a word in edgewise," said Prince Marvin. He was just about to laugh.

Then, for the first time ever, he thought what he'd said might not be funny. So he chewed his lip instead.

Princess Gusty Ox opened her mouth to call him Stink Brain. Then she closed her mouth again. She didn't want Godric the Geek to rule the kingdom.

She'd also noticed Marvin biting his lip and was glad that he had realized he should just be quiet.

Suddenly, a squirrel scampered along a branch above their heads. Just as it ducked to go into its hole, a pack of cards fell out of the hole. As the cards tumbled down through the branches, flashes of gold sparkled in its path!

Chapter Four

It was the final day of the challenge, and nothing was going right. No matter how hard Princess Gusty Ox and Prince Marvin tried not to fight, they just couldn't seem to stop themselves. Every game they played ended in a terrible argument.

First it was about card castles.

Prince Marvin said Princess Gusty Ox's castle didn't count because it was too wide at the bottom. Princess Gusty Ox said Prince Marvin's was no good because he used pinecone sap to stick the edges of his cards together.

Then they tried playing poker, betting with acorns, but that didn't work, either, because they both cheated too much. No matter what, they couldn't get along.

"How are we going to find the right game?" wailed Princess Gusty Ox.

Prince Marvin rolled on his back and kicked the air with his feet.

"What in the world is wrong with you?" asked Princess Gusty Ox.

"I'm starving!" yelled Prince Marvin. "I haven't eaten for days!"

Princess Gusty Ox put her hand inside her pocket. In it were some berries she had picked off a bush when her brother wasn't looking. Suddenly, it occurred to her that if they were going to win the challenge, they would have to help each other. She handed the berries to him.

Prince Marvin immediately stopped rolling. "Are you sure?" he muttered, barely able to meet his sister's eye.

Princess Gusty Ox nodded.

Prince Marvin was just about to swallow the handful in one gulp, but he changed his mind and gave some back to his sister. He thought she must be just as hungry as he was.

The prince and princess stared at each other. They knew they were both wondering the same thing: Why did they fight all of the time? It wasn't just about the kingdom. They'd fought since they were very young.

"I wonder if all brothers and sisters are like us," said Princess Gusty Ox.

"I don't know," replied Prince Marvin. He chewed his lip. "Father might know, but, like you said, he never talks to us."

"I don't think he likes us much," said Princess Gusty Ox.

Prince Marvin scratched the ground with his fingers. "We're not very nice to him, are we?" he asked.

"No," mumbled Princess Gusty Ox.

A gust of wind swirled around the bottom of the tree and lifted the cards into the air.

Princess Gusty Ox and Prince Marvin looked down. They both saw two queens facing upward. It seemed like the perfect time to play a game of Snap. Both of them smiled as they realized the opportunity.

"Snap!" they both yelled.

Then, they did something they hadn't ever done. They both burst out laughing at the same time. At that moment, the children picked up the cards and began to play.

It was the first time they had ever really enjoyed a game together, so they played over and over again. They were having such a good time, they didn't notice that the sun was sinking in the sky.

"Marv!" cried Princess Gusty Ox. She had recently promised never to call her brother Stink Brain again.

Prince Marvin looked up from his stack of cards and grinned. "What is it, Big G?" he asked. In return, he had promised to stop calling his sister Elephant Feet.

Princess Gusty Ox grinned and exclaimed, "I think we've found the right game! What do you think?"

"I think so, too!" Prince Marvin said as he grinned at his sister. "Let's go home!"

"Jump on my shoulders," said the princess. "It's the fastest way!" And they set off through the forest.

Chapter Five

King Cudgel woke to the strangest noise. At first, he didn't know what it was. Sometimes, it sounded like gurgling water in a creek. Other times, it sounded like a pigeon cooing or a rooster crowing.

The king moaned and pulled a pillow over his head. He knew it was impossible, but it almost sounded like children's laughter.

"Wake up! Wake up!" Quail skipped into the room balancing a tea tray on his head.

King Cudgel poked his nose over the bedsheets. "What's that noise?" he asked.

Quail placed the tray on a table, drew back the curtains, and opened the window. The noise was louder than ever.

"Princess Gusty Ox and Prince Marvin have returned, sire," answered Quail. "Look!

I've never seen anything like it!"

King Cudgel slid out of bed. He walked over to the window and peered outside. He grabbed a table to stop himself from fainting. His children were playing on a seesaw!

"When did they get back from their trip?" croaked King Cudgel.

"Early this morning, sire. They didn't want to disturb you," answered Quail.

King Cudgel felt a wave of dizziness wash over him. It was the first time his children had ever thought of anyone except themselves.

"Summon Crackle!" he cried. "He'll know what this means."

"Crackle has been summoned, sire," said Quail proudly. "I took the liberty myself."

As he spoke, he opened the king's closet and took out a pair of striped, velvet pants and a shirt embroidered with comets.

Then, he placed a pair of pointed shoes on the floor. They were teal and decorated with square, diamond buckles. They completed King Cudgel's party outfit, and Quail was certain there would be something to celebrate that day.

A moment later, Crackle floated into the room. He was so pleased with himself, he couldn't make his feet touch the ground.

"Crackle!" cried King Cudgel. He was looking out his window again. Now his children were playing Ping-Pong out in the castle yard. "What does this mean?"

"It means the steam never lies," replied Crackle, barely able to hide the triumph in his voice. "It means that your dear children have completed their challenge and learned a very important lesson. It means that now you can retire to the seaside."

"But what have they learned?" asked the king. Happy voices rang out from the courtyard below. "I don't understand."

"They have learned to get along with each other," explained Crackle. "They have learned that fighting is a waste of time."

"And not nice for anyone," added Quail.

"And not nice at all," agreed Crackle.

King Cudgel couldn't believe what he was hearing. "How long will it last?" he asked.

"Forever," replied Crackle. "Sire, as I predicted, your nightmares are now over." He bowed and waved his cape. "Now, if you'll excuse me, after all of this hard work, I'm going to sun my belly on a lily pad."

The king waved him away, and Crackle floated back through the open door. The room went silent. King Cudgel sat down on the edge of his bed.

He opened his emergency bedside chest and filled his mouth with sugar cubes. "Quail," he said in a trembling voice. "I don't know what to do."

Quail frowned and asked, "What is wrong now, sire?"

Princess Gusty Ox's voice rose through the air. "Great serve, Marv!" she exclaimed.

"Fabulous rally, Big G!" Marvin replied.

They laughed, and the sharp tapping of the Ping-Pong ball started up again.

King Cudgel groaned and held his head. "I never believed they would ever stop fighting," he said. "That's why I wanted to retire to the seaside."

"I guessed as much," said Quail. "And now you would like to change your mind?"

King Cudgel looked up. His eyes were bright. "Do you think I could, Quail? I mean, it's not too late, is it?"

"You are the king, sire," replied Quail. "You can do what you want."

He picked up the party clothes and began placing them at the end of the bed.

Quail added, "And I think you'll find that the prince and princess will be very happy if you stay here, too."

King Cudgel walked over to the window. Beyond the meadows, the hills were as green as emeralds, and the forest was alive with singing birds. Crunchbone Castle was the loveliest place in the world.

Fluffy ran to the door and began barking as Princess Gusty Ox and Prince Marvin walked into the room.

King Cudgel couldn't believe it. Their
eyes were shining, and their cheeks were
pink. But best of all were the smiles that
spread across their faces.

"Congratulations!" cried King Cudgel.
"I'm very proud of you!"

Even Quail had to wipe a tear from his
eye as Princess Gusty Ox and Prince Marvin
ran into their father's arms.

King Cudgel hugged his children as hard as he could. "We're going to be a real family from now on and live happily ever after," he whispered. He gave them both an extra squeeze. "And just so you know, I think Godric the Geek is the most boring person in the kingdom, too!"

On the Web

FactHound offers a safe, fun way to find Web sites related to topics in this book. All of the sites on FactHound have been researched by our staff.

1. Visit *www.facthound.com*
2. Type in this special code:
   140483706X
3. Click on the FETCH IT button.

Your trusty FactHound will fetch the best sites for you!